Rocky Mountain Rabbit

By
BECKY WOODS

Illustrated by *SARAH WOODS*

A WINDSWEPT BOOK
Windswept House
Mt. Desert, Maine

10   9   8   7   6   5   4   3

Printed in the United States of America
for the Publisher by
Downeast Graphics & Printing, Inc.
Ellsworth, Maine

To
David, Heather, Jason, Derrick & Lauren

The children that inspire
each moment of every day

A ROCKY MOUNTAIN FOREST slowly woke from winter's slumber, shoots of new vegetation poking tender green heads through the barren ground, as a pair of cottontail rabbits shuffled through the dry pine needles that carpeted the forest floor. They nibbled hungrily on the young plants that were just emerging, having recently endured the hunger that often comes with winter's harshness. The soft, grayish-brown rabbits welcomed spring's promise of abundance and though a few shaded spots still harbored shrunken, dirt encrusted snowdrifts, spring was surely erasing any signs of winter.

Sylvi, the female rabbit, was the larger of the pair, and seemed to be leading her mate. Occasionally she paused to eat the young shoots at her feet, but only for a short time, an anxious intuition telling her not to delay. Agus, her mate, lingered over the new grasses, not sharing his mate's nervous urge to move on. At one point he lifted his head for a momentary check, moving his ears forward and looking for danger in all directions. He noticed his impatient mate was leaving him behind, so reluctantly, Agus quit grazing to follow her lead.

Sylvi eventually led Agus to an abandoned badger hole that she had discovered a few days earlier. After inspecting the premises closely, making sure it was indeed vacant, Sylvi began clearing old sticks and debris from inside. She worked quickly, urgently, her nesting instinct driving her on. Agus helped, but he was not so intent as his mate and stopped at times to rest and nibble on nearby plants. Sylvi, driven by an inner sense, kept working intensely, tirelessly to finish their home in time.

When the hole had been cleared thoroughly enough to suit Sylvi, she moved outside and began to gather soft, dry grasses in her mouth. These she brought into the den where she used her feet and mouth to arrange them into a cozy nest. After several trips outside and much rearranging, Sylvi was finally satisfied and ready to put the finishing touches on her nest. She began to pull soft fur from her stomach with her teeth, placing it carefully in the nest to form a downy lining. Inspecting the nest carefully one last time, and feeling confident that it would meet her needs, Sylvi left the hole and entered the bright outdoors to wait.

Sylvi relaxed under the branches of a large bush, drawing her front paws under her chest and laying her ears along the back of her neck while the morning sun bathed her in its rays. She would use this waiting time to regain the strength she had exerted building the nest. She knew she would need it soon.

Agus noticed Sylvi and hopped toward her gingerly, his white puff of a tail moving rapidly from side to side, but Sylvi was exhausted and blinked her eyes at him sleepily. Unperturbed by Sylvi's lack of enthusiasm, Agus began to lick her affectionately. Sylvi closed her eyes and enjoyed the grooming.

CHAPTER 2

**YLVI AND AGUS** waited outside the new den for the rest of that day and through the night that followed. Early the next morning, while the sky was still pink with sunrise, Sylvi rose and entered the den. She knew it was time. Agus was absorbed in grazing near a large boulder several feet away and didn't seem to notice her departure.

Sylvi had been gone only a short time when Agus heard a scratching noise and glanced up to see a raccoon climbing backwards down the trunk of a nearby tree, scraping the bark with long, sharp claws. Once on the ground, the raccoon lumbered slowly toward the rabbit's den. Although raccoons are normally not much of a threat to rabbits, being too lazy to eat anything they have to chase, Agus realized that right now his mate was quite vulnerable. He was aware that Sylvi had quietly entered the den to give birth. In her present condition, she would be easy prey for the raccoon and newly born, defenseless babies would most surely be killed. Agus rushed toward the den, ready to fight any intruder in order to protect his family. The spunky little rabbit wouldn't back down even though the raccoon was almost twenty pounds heavier than he and had sharp teeth to match a sometimes vicious temperament. Luckily, the restless raccoon didn't even seem to notice Agus or his den as she waddled past. Agus was glad to see the bushy, ringed tail fade into the distance.

When Sylvi again emerged from the den, the sun had risen and a golden glow had replaced the pink hues in the sky. She was unaware of how close danger had come while she had been inside the den. Now she was overcome with fatigue and needed rest. Nevertheless, Sylvi stayed alert to any hint of an approaching enemy. She would now guard the den with her life.

The reason for Sylvi's intense protectiveness lay sleeping in the nest inside the abandoned badger hole. While she had been inside the den, Sylvi had given birth to five tiny bunnies. They were born hairless with smooth, loose skin. Tiny ears were folded flat against their heads and their eyelids were sealed tightly shut. At this point they bore no resemblance to their soft, furry parents.

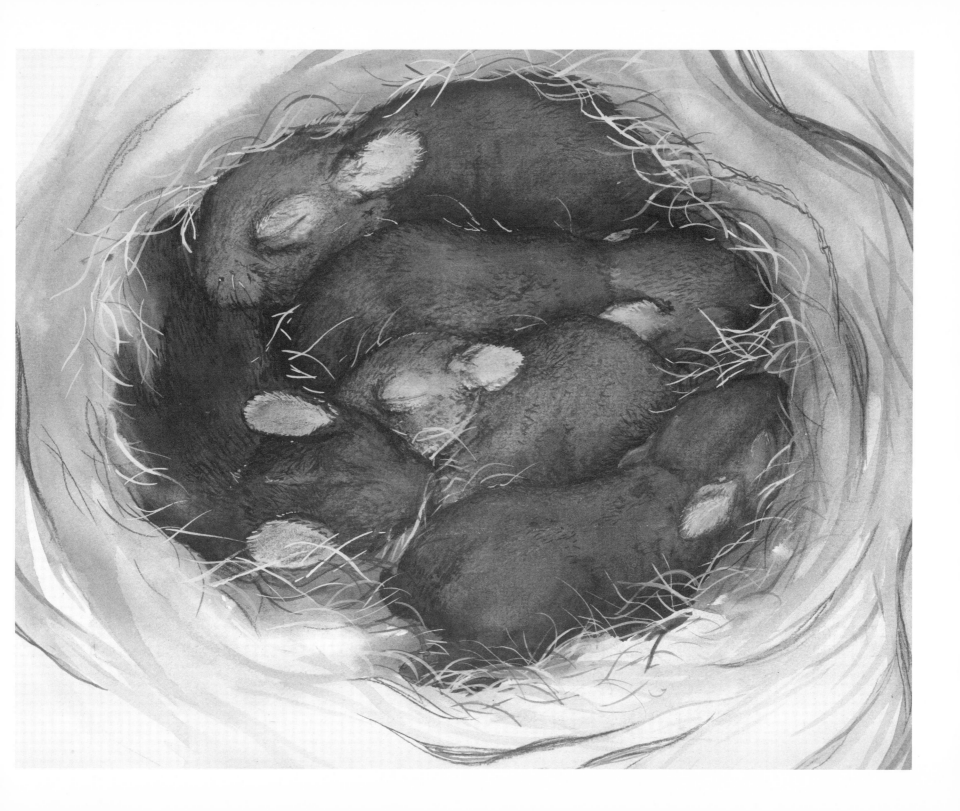

These blind, defenseless babies were completely dependent upon Sylvi's care for their survival. She had carefully covered them with fur from the nest before leaving them to come outside. This fur would keep their hairless bodies warm and because it was torn from her own stomach, the babies would be able to smell her comforting scent upon it. The babies would be reassured by the familiar scent and feel as though their mother were near even when she was away from the nest.

CHAPTER 3

ONE OF THE PINK BABIES snuggled into the soft nest that Sylvi had prepared was Vila. As she squirmed among the warm bodies in the nest, Vila noticed that one little form felt quite cold. She crawled closer to it. Although she couldn't see, Vila could feel that this body was also much tinier than the others in the nest. She snuggled closer to her cold sibling, trying to warm the frail bunny with her own body heat.

The little runt was Vila's sister, Nutta. She was much smaller than the other bunnies, perhaps too small to survive. Without the extra body heat that she received from her sister, Nutta would surely have perished within the first couple of hours after birth.

The other occupants of the nest were Tali, Vila's sister, the largest of the bunnies, and their two brothers, Cotton and Otto. After napping for some time, the bunnies began to wake, receiving messages from their tummies that it was time to eat. Soon a new source of warmth radiated over them and they became excited as they sensed the presence of their mother. Although they couldn't see her, instinct told the bunnies to crawl toward her to satisfy their pangs of hunger, all of the bunnies but Nutta. The weak little runt still slept.

Vila felt Tali climb over her, anxious to reach their mother's warm, nourishing milk. Cotton and Otto also began to nurse. Vila nudged Nutta, finally waking her small sister. Nutta crawled weakly to their mother and made a feeble attempt to eat. Even though she was too weak to nurse for long, her mother's milk was very rich. Perhaps it would give her strength enough to survive until her next feeding.

When the babies had finished nursing, Sylvi began to lick them gently. This kept their bodies clean, and as her tongue gently massaged their fat little tummies, it helped the meal they had just eaten digest. Vila felt full and satisfied. Her mother's presence filled her with a sense of contentment, and soon Vila joined her brothers and sisters who had already fallen asleep. Sylvi carefully covered the babies with fur from the nest, her large, brown eyes reflecting the special concern that is a mother's love.

CHAPTER 4

**D**URING THE NEXT WEEK, the bunnies changed greatly. They grew soft, fuzzy fur. Small ears stood up from round heads and white pom-pom tails protruded behind round, soft bodies. The bunnies were now fluffy miniatures of their parents.

Little Nutta still clung to life, although she remained small and thin, appearing bony and rather scraggly. She still slept more than the other bunnies, but Vila stayed near her frail sister, waking her to eat and snuggling close to keep her warm. At these times, Nutta would cuddle close to Vila, giving her warm affectionate licks with her small tongue.

One morning Vila awoke to find a wonderful change in her world: it was no longer dark. Her eyes had opened! She could see the brothers and sisters that she had shared the nest with since birth and when Sylvi came to the nest to feed them their warm breakfast, Vila was finally able to see the mother that she loved so much. She found this love reflected back at her from the soft, round eyes of her mother.

Vila watched as her mother moved one large ear slightly forward and jumped into the nest to join her anxiously waiting babies.

After breakfast, Sylvi tried to bathe the bunnies, but they were so excited over their new sense of sight they could barely hold still. Fuzzy, white, powder-puff tails bounced through the air as the bunnies jumped about playfully. Now, large, soft eyes nearly filled their round faces, giving them a look of sweet innocence.

Sylvi endured the antics of her gleeful young for a time before her patience began to wear thin. Finally, she made a low, grunting sound and nosed the playful babies into the nest. Nutta was already there, curled into a tiny ball, sleeping soundly. Soon her exhausted brothers and sisters joined her, the five of them forming a single ball of fur.

Sylvi left her sleeping babies and went outside to join Agus. She no longer bothered to cover the babies with fur as they now had plenty of their own to keep them warm until her return.

CHAPTER 5

NE MORNING, as every morning, the bunnies anxiously watched for the shadow that passed across the den entrance, announcing the arrival of their mother as her body momentarily blocked the sun's rays. When the familiar shadow appeared, the hungry bunnies scampered to greet their mother. Tali pushed ahead of the rest, followed closely by Cotton and Otto. Vila waited for Nutta before bouncing after them.

Suddenly Tali came to an abrupt halt. Cotton and Otto froze in their tracks behind her. Vila and Nutta knew something must be wrong, so they inched forward cautiously. An unfamiliar scent filled the den and Vila looked ahead to see a strange rabbit standing between them and the entrance. Nutta turned and raced to the shelter of the nest in alarm. The rest of the bunnies stayed still, frozen with fear.

The strange rabbit came toward the frightened bunnies. He reached Tali and began to sniff her. Tali crouched down, too frightened to move. The strange rabbit rubbed his chin over Tali's head and ears. He moved forward and did the same to

Cotton, Otto, and Vila, who were also too afraid to move. The rabbit was leaving a special scent from his chin glands on them, marking them as his own. The bunnies had just met their father.

Another shadow crossed the den. This time it was the bunnies' mother. She came in quietly and moved forward, past Agus. Seeing her mother gave little Nutta the courage to venture out of the nest again. She raced to her mother's side, seeking protection between her mother's front legs. Agus came toward them. Nutta tried to burrow further beneath her mother, peeking only her nose out from between Sylvi's front legs. Agus reached his nose toward Nutta and gently sniffed her. Relaxing somewhat, Nutta inched forward and put her tiny nose against her father's larger one. Agus licked his tiniest offspring with a scratchy tongue, then rubbed his chin across her head, marking her as his, also.

Now that the introductions were over, Sylvi settled down to the business of nursing her hungry babies. They lay on their backs and reached to her warm stomach for breakfast. Agus lay at the den opening, watching and enjoying his family.

CHAPTER 6

SUALLY, SYLVI TUCKED her full, satisfied babies into their nest for a nap after they had eaten and been given their morning bath. However, this morning was different. This morning Sylvi encouraged her babies to follow as she and Agus left the den.

Tali hurried out, close on her mother's heels. Cotton, Otto, Vila, and Nutta followed behind her excitedly, but at the entrance little Nutta lost her courage. She was afraid to leave the den. Warily, she stuck her head out, only to retreat inside at the slightest movement or sound.

Once outside, the other bunnies also became more cautious. This was a strange, new world they were entering. The sky was endless and there were no protective walls or boundaries as there were in their familiar burrow. Sylvi and Agus showed their babies how to nibble tender shoots of grass that grew nearby, but more importantly, they taught them to watch constantly for danger.

As always, Tali was the first to feel brave and adventurous. She began to explore by sniffing around the trunk of a nearby pine tree. Thin spikes of grass tickled her nose and made her whiskers twitch.

Cotton and Otto preferred to hide under the protective branches of a nearby bush, coming out to eat the tender grass that grew all about them only when they felt certain no danger was lurking near.

For a time, Vila stayed near the entrance of the den, hoping to coax Nutta out, but she gave up and ran to join Tali when she saw how much fun her sister was having. Tali lunged into the air, kicking her hind feet up behind her. Vila ran toward Tali at top speed and leapt right over her sister's head. The two sisters had a great time frisking in the warm sunshine until a dark shadow blocked the golden rays of sun and cast a dark form onto the ground in front of them.

The menacing shadow scared the two frolicking bunnies who immediately raced to the safety of their den. They could move quite fast now and they did! Cotton and Otto also saw the shadow as it slithered across the ground. They sped into the den right behind Tali and Vila, not stopping until they were safely burrowed into the familiar nest.

Nutta was startled as her brothers and sisters burst into the nest in a panic. The frightened bunnies huddled together, shaking with fright. Vila could feel her heart pounding heavily in her chest. Maybe outside wasn't the wonderful place it had seemed at first.

When the bunnies were sure the shadow hadn't followed into the den, they calmed down and eventually fell asleep, totally exhausted. None of them ventured outside again that day, not even the brave Tali. They had all learned a valuable lesson in survival, even though they didn't know the shadow that had frightened them so badly was only that of a friendly robin flying overhead. Next time it could be a larger, more threatening bird of prey.

CHAPTER 7

**FTER THEIR FIRST ADVENTURE** outdoors, Sylvi allowed the bunnies to come and go as they wished and now the family wandered farther from the den area. Sometimes they visited a special place where the forest drew back like a giant curtain revealing a large, open meadow. Gentle breezes rustled through springtime flowers, transforming the meadow into a swaying basket of fragrant color. Many of the flowers that grew in the meadow were favorite foods of the rabbits.

One morning the family slowly made their way to the meadow, stopping at several places to nibble plants, grazing as they went. The bunnies could always sense an extra alertness about their parents when in the meadow, its openness offering no protection, making the rabbits easy prey.

In the meadow, the bunnies played near the edge, jumping about, releasing some of their boundless energy. While the large pines of the forest filtered the sunlight and kept the forest floor shady and cool, the morning sun bathed the open meadow in an unbroken shower of rays. The golden light seemed to feed and increase the babies' energy, and they jumped and frolicked, drifting into a magical world all their own. Suddenly, vibrations moving along the ground shattered the walls of fantasy and brought the bunnies abruptly back to reality. Sylvi and Agus were thumping a signal of danger with their large hind feet that vibrated along the ground to their young. The baby rabbits knew this signal well. It meant there was a very real threat close by.

Vila's ears perked up and her eyes darted about, trying to locate the danger. It didn't take long for her to spot it. A hungry-looking coyote was stealthily sneaking through the long grasses on the meadow's edge, closing in on the rabbits.

Vila's eyes darted ahead of the coyote and that was when she saw Nutta. The tiny bunny had wandered from the others and now she was frozen in terror directly in the path of the coyote. Vila hoped desperately that the coyote hadn't seen Nutta crouched motionless in the grass only a few feet in front of it. Instinct had told the baby rabbit to freeze, and with luck, the enemy would pass without noticing her. However, luck didn't seem to be with Nutta as the coyote stalked toward her, ears perked forward, eyes riveted on the spot where she crouched. The coyote appeared ready to pounce and Vila feared her tiny sister would be killed at any moment. She turned her eyes away, not bearing to watch it happen to this little rabbit who had struggled so hard just to survive.

Then, realizing the coyote had seen her, Nutta reacted, and again instinct dictated what she should do. Since she couldn't hide, the little rabbit screeched loudly, causing Vila to again look toward the meadow and causing the coyote to back up a step. It was only a step, but it threw the coyote off long enough for the fast little bunny to streak across the meadow.

Nutta ran for the shelter of the forest, the quickest route bringing her directly toward Vila, with the quick coyote following closely after her. No longer merely a spectator, Vila turned and raced back into the forest with Nutta and the coyote right behind her. Remembering having recently played close by in a hollow beneath a large boulder, Vila turned sharply and changed direction, seeking the refuge of the rock. She was relieved when she saw it just ahead, and in a moment the two fat little

bunnies were squeezing their bodies under the space beneath the heavy boulder. The coyote was much too large to fit into the opening, so she reached into it with her front paws. The bunnies pressed as close to the back of the rock as they could. Luckily, the coyote's legs weren't long enough to reach them.

Although her heart was pounding and her body heaved with heavy, frightened breaths, Vila began to relax a bit as she realized the coyote couldn't reach them. Then, suddenly, her fear returned and her heart began to race again when she saw the coyote had begun to dig at the dirt with her sharp forepaws. Vila knew it was only a matter of time before the coyote would dig an opening large enough to reach her paws into.

As Vila tried to decide what to do next, the coyote suddenly quit digging and lifted her head, looking behind her. Her mate was calling to her from the middle of the meadow. The female glanced back down at the opening, paused for a moment, and then decided to give up on the rabbits, for today anyway. She turned toward the meadow and her waiting mate. Vila and Nutta watched from their hiding place as the coyote loped off, her long, bushy tail wagging in greeting to the waiting male. The coyotes were leaving, but they probably had a den full of hungry pups in the area. They would surely be a threat to the rabbits again.

Vila and Nutta stayed hidden for a time, until their breathing and heartbeats had slowed to normal. Vila poked her head out, and seeing no immediate danger, slowly inched her entire body from beneath the rock. She stood on her hind legs and surveyed the area thoroughly, trying to convince Nutta that the danger had passed. Finally, she too, came out of hiding. Soon the two little bunnies were racing up the trail, back to the safety of their home and parents.

In the nest, Vila snuggled close to her mother. Sylvi's tongue caressed her with warm reassurances. Vila felt that nothing could ever harm her as long as she was close enough to hear the comforting beat of her mother's heart pulsing in her ears. Vila closed her eyes and fell into a contented sleep, the love of her mother falling over her like a comforting blanket.

CHAPTER 8

HE YOUNG RABBITS began to spend more and more time away from their parents. As they ate more grasses and plants their bodies required less of their mother's milk. By the time they were three weeks old, they no longer needed to nurse, although little Nutta still tried to at times. Nutta was seeking comfort and security at these times, rather than nourishment, and Sylvi would jump away from her angrily. She knew it was time to discourage babyish habits, time for the bunnies to learn to survive on their own.

One gray and misty morning, Vila and Nutta went to the meadow for breakfast. After they had been there only a short time, the sky opened up to release a heavy downpour of rain. The two bunnies quickly ran toward the shelter of the dry den.

As they neared the den, Sylvi, who had been unusually nervous for a few days now, ran forward angrily. Vila thought that Sylvi must be uneasy about the rain and tried to run past her mother into the nice, dry den. Now Sylvi hopped in front of her and a low growl warned Vila to stop. As she looked past her mother, into the den, Vila could see that the nest inside was carefully covered with soft fur. Now Vila began to understand her mother's behavior. Sylvi must have given birth to a new litter of bunnies while she and Nutta had been in the meadow. Sylvi was protecting THEM now. Vila and Nutta would no longer be allowed inside the den.

Rather than stand where they were and be further drenched by the rain that pelted their coats, the two rejected bunnies hurried down the path in search of shelter. They found it under a pile of large boulders. The leaves of nearby bushes acted as tiny umbrellas to cover the crevices and keep the cave beneath dry.

Once inside, Nutta began to groom Vila's wet coat with her tongue. Vila barely noticed. She was looking longingly up the path toward her mother, knowing she could go to her only with her eyes. She could see Sylvi resting in the form she had made by pushing the long grasses down into a bed. Her ears were laid back and her body was tense, ready to defend her new babies. Vila was sad when she remembered that not so long ago she had been one of the babies that Sylvi had watched over so carefully.

As Vila continued to watch the path outside, she saw Cotton and Otto run down it, toward the den. They were followed by Tali who was also seeking shelter from the rain. The three of them were greeted as Vila and Nutta had been. Sylvi jumped from the form she rested in to chase them away. They ran down the path and disappeared under the protective branches of some thick brush.

Vila was grateful for the company and warmth her little sister provided, but still her heart ached. The cave filled with sadness as the young rabbits realized their mother was lost to them forever. Never again would they smell her familiar scent close by or feel the reassuring beat of her heart in their ears. The thought that made them feel the most frightened and alone was knowing they would have to care for themselves now without their mother's protection.

Nutta burrowed her nose into Vila's fur. She needed the comfort of her sister's closeness more than ever now.

Outside, the rain continued to fall. The sky remained dark and the day had become even more gloomy. Although Vila felt grateful for the dryness of the cave, she couldn't help wishing she were back in Sylvi's den. At least she still had Nutta to snuggle close to — which she did.

CHAPTER 9

AS SUMMER WORE ON, Vila and Nutta grew steadily closer. They were more alone now than ever before. They had lost their sister. One dark night, a large owl had swooped down on hushed wings and grabbed Tali in his sharp talons. Because owls' feathers are designed for silent flight, the unsuspecting rabbit had no warning of her impending doom. Vila missed her bold, pushy sister. Hungry predators lurked everywhere and the number of rabbits in the area became fewer and fewer.

Cotton and Otto had left the area, causing Vila and Nutta to feel even more lonely. The male rabbits had become old enough for Agus to look upon them as rivals, so they had spread out to establish territories of their own.

Vila became more and more aware of the dangers that were all around her. She was glad that Nutta was with her so she didn't have to face these dangers alone. Likewise, Nutta was reassured by the presence of the big sister that had always watched over her.

The rabbits would soon be facing another danger, the weather. As summer became fall, the days grew shorter. The green border of aspen trees that grew along the stream had changed to blazing gold. Leaves everywhere followed suit, becoming gold and orange and red before drying, turning brown, and falling to the forest floor. Only skeletons of the leafy green trees of summer remained. Needles of evergreens provided the only green that remained in the forest.

One afternoon, following a dark and gloomy morning, the first snow began to fall. Soft clouds rose from the horizon, turning the sky milky white. At first, this milky sky spat only a few large, white flakes, but soon they increased and became a solid, snowy wall that cascaded down from above. By dusk the earth was blanketed with a four inch carpet of white.

Vila and Nutta had never seen snow before. They spent the afternoon watching it fall from the safety of their cave. At dusk, they ventured out into the strange, white stuff, cautiously testing it with one front paw. After shaking the snow from their paws several times, the two rabbits overcame their fear and soon they were leaping through it playfully.

Most of this first snow melted off quickly, clearing areas where the rabbits could find food. There were several more of these short-lived snow storms before winter's first ferocious blizzard occurred.

CHAPTER 10

INTER'S FIRST BLIZZARD began early in the morning with heavy snowflakes falling gently to earth. Then the wind began to blow, slowly and quietly at first, gradually becoming stronger and louder. As the wind gained speed, it began to howl and swirl snow in every direction. Vila and Nutta ran for the protection of their cave as the cold, wet snow whipped around them. They stayed in their shelter for two days, listening to the merciless howl of the wind outside. The hungry rabbits dug in the dirt beneath them finding roots from the surrounding bushes to eat. The cave became dark as the savage wind piled snow into high drifts that blocked the cave entrance. The two rabbits huddled close together, trying to keep warm as frigid air penetrated the walls of their home. They were eventually lulled to sleep by the steady roar of the wind outside.

While the rabbits slept, the storm played itself out and the wind ceased blowing. When Vila and Nutta woke, silence filled their cave. Vila scurried to the entrance and began to dig out of the snow covered cave. Nutta pitched in, helping to remove snow with her front paws. After clearing a tunnel to the outside, the rabbits stuck their heads out for a quick look around. A still, white world lay before them. The temperature was well below zero, and the clear, quiet air seemed alive with the bright sparkle of dancing ice crystals. Snow rested on the branches of the forest trees, changing even the evergreens to white. This bright, glimmering forest was beautiful, but the air was so icy cold that the rabbits' nostrils stuck together with every breath.

The stream where Vila and Nutta drank had frozen into solid ice beneath a thick blanket of snow. The rabbits would have to melt the snow in their mouths if they were thirsty. Finding food wasn't going to be quite so easy. Vila couldn't see any plants that weren't covered with snow.

The rabbits weren't the only animals struggling to find food. As Vila and Nutta hopped lightly over the white ground, they noticed deep depressions in the snow. These prints had been made by the paws of an animal heavier than themselves, paws that had sunk into the snow, past the top crust that supported the rabbits. Vila and Nutta sniffed the large footprints, their keen noses recognizing the scent of bobcat. The large cat was hunting beyond his normal boundaries. Winter's harshness would bring many hungry enemies, searching for food, into the rabbits' territory.

As winter tightened its grip on the forest, Vila and Nutta clung to each other for the strength to continue the struggle for survival. Living through winter's harshness was a great challenge, requiring much strength and courage.

Vila and Nutta had to wander quite far from home searching for food. One night as yellow light from the moon and stars reflected off the snow with a sparkling brilliance, they found a group of bushes that had been cleared of snow by the wind. A steep snowdrift had piled up forming a wall around the bushes. The hungry rabbits slid down the drift, and began to eat eagerly.

Hidden behind the snowdrift, Vila and Nutta had focused their attention on eating. Perhaps that was why they were unaware of a night time hunter who stalked them stealthily. The hunter was a twenty pound feline, many times the size of the small rabbits. His face was surrounded by a ruff of fur and pointed tufts of hair stuck up from his ears. His tail was a six inch stub — the rabbits were being stalked by a hungry bobcat.

The cat inched forward slowly, quietly, until he reached the drift. Then in a sudden rush, he attacked, leaping over the snowdrift and hurling himself at the rabbits as they grazed.

The rabbits' sensitive ears heard the rustle in the air as the cat hurled toward them. Just before he landed, Vila leapt to one side, and Nutta to the other, both out of the feline's reach. Then Vila ran with lightning speed in one direction while Nutta ran with equal speed in the opposite direction. The bobcat pursued Vila.

Vila ran across the crusted snow for what seemed like hours. Although she was lighter than the cat and could run over the snow with more ease, Vila was also hungry and tired. She didn't know how much longer she could continue to run. Up ahead she saw a large dead tree lying on the ground. Knowing that her strength was about to give out, Vila squeezed under the massive trunk, hoping the cat wouldn't be able to move the heavy tree.

The bobcat did try to roll the trunk over, but it was frozen down and heavy, and he was too hungry to wait around for the rabbit to come out. He left Vila to resume his hunt.

Vila stayed under the log 'til daybreak. All through the night she worried, wondering if Nutta were allright. She wasn't sure her little sister could survive without her and she knew that she felt much braver and more sure of herself when she was with Nutta. The song of the forest birds filled the morning air. There was no alarm in their song, so Vila knew it was safe to come out. She must begin the long trip home to find Nutta.

 **ILA BEGAN THE JOURNEY** home. She had just wound her way around several tall trees that blocked her path when her sensitive ears picked up the sound of movement close by. She stopped and stood on her hind legs, hoping to see the source of the sound. Her long ears continually moved forward and back, listening. All Vila could hear was the gentle rustle of pine boughs as they swayed in the wind, so she lowered her paws back to the ground.

Only a few feet away, cleverly hidden behind a large tree trunk, a red fox had been watching Vila's progress. It was his movements that Vila had heard. As she stood looking around on her hind legs, the fox had frozen behind the tree, not moving a muscle or making a sound. When he saw Vila relax and lower her front paws, the fox had crouched low, then lunged. His red fur and white tail blurred together as he hurled himself through the air toward the little rabbit. As he landed, the fox tried to pin Vila under his front paws. Vila was fast enough to scramble from under his grasp; however, she wasn't quite fast enough to escape his snapping teeth.

The fox had grabbed Vila's hind leg in his mouth just as she jumped away. While pulling her leg free, Vila had scraped it against the sharp teeth of the fox, causing a bad tear. Both fur and skin had been ripped back, exposing raw flesh and bone.

The pain in Vila's leg caused her to become confused, it was almost unbearable. She didn't know which way to run, and she could barely move her injured leg.

It took only a moment for the fox to catch up to Vila. He jumped in front of her teasingly, feeling confident the rabbit had no hope of escape. Not being particularly hungry at the moment, the fox began to "play" with his prey. He hopped lightly over the pathetic little rabbit, nipping at her playfully as he jumped back and forth. Vila winced as the sharp teeth of the fox bit into one of her ears.

Vila was exhausted and frightened. The pain in her leg was beginning to take control. She felt so alone, and without even Nutta to turn to Vila didn't know what to do except give up.

As she watched the fox advance, jaws open wide, Vila became a shivering ball of surrendering fur. Then from deep within her, an undiscovered inner strength began to surface, causing Vila to feel something other than despair. Suddenly Vila knew it didn't matter if she was alone because she was the one in control of her will to survive, and she couldn't give up on herself.

Now Vila was filled with a new determination, and as the confident fox advanced she made a last desperate move. Filled with new courage, Vila ignored the excruciating pain in her leg and used her remaining strength to spring past the open jaws of the fox. She began to limp up the path, dragging her injured leg behind her. Some thick bushes full of dense undergrowth lay ahead. Vila could run no further, she knew this would have to do. The fatigued rabbit wiggled into the thick brush.

The fox had been surprised and caught off guard when the prey he thought was through fighting had suddenly sprung away from him. The surprise made him a little slow to react, but when he did he came after Vila in a fury. As Vila pulled herself further into the thick brush, the fox began digging his way into the thick, thorn-filled undergrowth after her. Vila refused to give up now and wormed her small body deeper and deeper into the tangled undergrowth of the thicket.

The larger fox was beginning to struggle as thorns caught at his long fur, tangling and pulling at it. Before long he had to turn back, inching his way back out of the thicket. When the fox finally managed to untangle himself from the thorny maze, he laid down in front of the bushes and began to groom his coat. After his grooming, the fox stretched out and napped.

Perhaps the fox was only pretending to sleep, a ruse to lure Vila out of hiding. If so, he would have to keep up the pretense for quite some time because Vila was hurt badly, too badly to come out of the brush any time soon. Her leg would require much rest in order to heal. Luckily, the tear in her ear was fairly small and would mend more quickly. Vila carefully licked her injured leg, then collapsed into an exhausted heap and slept.

CHAPTER 12

**ILA STAYED HIDDEN** in the thicket for many days. She nibbled on the branches that were all around her when she felt hungry. Vila's thoughts often turned to Nutta, and she wondered if her sister had been able to reach home safely. Vila was afraid she would never again see the little sister who had always been so close to her.

During the second night in the thicket, a wet spring snow began to fall on Vila through holes in the branches above, soaking her fur. She curled into a damp, shivering ball. As night fell, so did the temperature, causing Vila's bloody leg to throb with pain. Her wet fur began to freeze. The miserable little rabbit eventually fell into a feverish, pain filled sleep while the frigid wind howled through the branches all around her.

The weather stayed cold and gloomy for several days. More wet snow fell daily and the winds were brisk and cold. Vila stayed huddled under the moist branches, cold and chilled, but not yet strong enough to go in search of drier quarters. She was waging a desperate battle just to stay alive and not give in to the pain and cold that threatened to consume her body. Once a family of mice scampered past her. They were so busy looking for food they hardly noticed the sick rabbit. Vila felt very alone.

The sunshine of a warm spring day finally dawned, coaxing Vila out. Her leg hurt as she slowly dragged herself forward, but Vila could tell that even though it was stiff, her leg was beginning to heal and grow stronger. She wouldn't be able to run for quite some time though and would be very easy prey for predators in her crippled condition.

Vila's injured leg kept her close to the thicket for the next few weeks. New plant shoots were beginning to push through the earth, making Vila grateful for the fresh, close food. Springtime was making her anxious to be on her way home, but she knew she hadn't recovered enough strength to leave the safety of the thicket. Vila was becoming desperately lonely.

A sunny morning found her lazily stretched out in front of the thicket, warm rays of sunshine penetrating her fur and warming her, and causing her to doze. Vila was watching the clearing in front of her with half-closed eyes when she saw the grass across the clearing move. She jumped up, suddenly alert, her lazy mood abandoned. Vila's nose and whiskers twitched and her long ears moved back and

forth quickly. The slight movement now became a shape as something came out of the grass and into the open. Vila was ready to retreat into the protection of the thicket when she realized the shape was that of another rabbit.

The visitor hadn't spotted Vila as she stood motionless watching him. He was busily nibbling new shoots, but suddenly lifted his head as though sensing he was being watched. His round, dark eyes rose to meet Vila's. Vila didn't move so the new rabbit came forward slowly until he was only inches from Vila. She cautiously moved toward him to sniff noses. Vila liked this new rabbit immediately, and it wasn't long before her feeling of loneliness had completely vanished.

Tona, the new rabbit didn't leave, but stayed in the thicket with Vila. Vila's leg had almost completely healed now and she had recovered most of her strength and speed, but she would not return to her old home. She would make a new one here with Tona.

The pair of rabbits discovered an abandoned hole on the other side of the thicket which they claimed. They began to clear old debris from inside the hole. This new den would fill the need Vila now felt for a place that was safe and secure.

Although Vila was happy and satisfied with her new life, she felt sad that she would never again see her sweet little sister.

CHAPTER 13

**PRINGTIME BECAME SUMMER** and beautiful wildflowers through out the forest opened their buds to show off colorful blossoms. Early one morning, when the sky was still an early morning shade of pink, Vila and Tona went to a nearby clearing to graze. Except for the ever present song of the forest birds, all was quiet. Inspired by the beginning of such a lovely day, Vila and Tona became restless. Instead of feeding in the familiar clearing as they usually did, they scampered past it to explore new places.

The playful rabbits chased each other to the top of a small rise. From there they could see an inviting meadow nestled in the valley below. Always cautious, Vila and Tona looked all around, then, seeing no danger, they bounded down the sloping hill to the valley floor.

The rabbits hadn't been in the meadow long when the sound of something rustling in the bushes across the meadow reached Vila's ears. She looked to the opposite edge of the clearing just as a family of baby bunnies emerged from the cover of brush that grew on their side of the meadow. The bunnies were very small, this was most likely their first trip to the meadow. Vila watched the bunnies as they played and she remembered how, long ago, she had played with her sisters and brothers in a meadow not so different from this one.

Vila could also see rabbits, a buck and a doe, resting under the branches of a bush near the playful bunnies. Their ears and eyes were alert, watching for anything that might threaten their young family. Suddenly, both the mother and the father sat upright, defensive and tense. They had noticed Vila and Tona across the meadow.

Vila observed the distant doe as she looked about nervously, and something in her movements seemed familiar to Vila. Once again her mind returned to that long ago meadow in her past. The memory of a loving playmate in another meadow in another time flooded Vila's mind and filled an empty spot in her heart. The vision of her sister traveled back with Vila from the past to the present. Then past and present seemed to blend together as Vila focused on the doe across the meadow. Nutta! The doe that had caused so many long forgotten memories to flow into Vila's mind was Nutta!

Nutta had been watching Vila also, and the two recognized each other at the same instant. Each rabbit bounded from her edge of the meadow, racing toward the center where the two met for a joyful reunion. Vila felt as though she had found a missing part of herself. She had spent so many hours wondering what had become of Nutta and now here she was, safe and happy. The sisters nuzzled each other joyously, staying close together, both finding it hard to believe they had really found one another again.

Vila and Tona spent a little more time in the meadow with Nutta and her mate, watching over Nutta's frolicking babies, but they knew they must return to their own home. They would meet Nutta and her family in the lush meadow again.

After sniffing noses to say good-bye, Vila and Tona scampered off toward their own den. Vila was filled with happiness now that she had actually seen Nutta, yet she could hardly wait to return to her own home and make sure all was as she had left it.

Relief washed over Vila as she entered the den and saw that the nest she had left earlier that morning was still carefully covered with soft fur. The four tiny bunnies she had nursed and carefully bathed hours before were still sleeping soundly. They began to stir as Vila came closer, the familiar scent and warmth of their mother radiating toward them. The helpless babies snuggled close to her. Vila looked down at them tenderly, knowing she would need every ounce of the new strength and courage she had found within herself to protect and teach these newest bunnies of the forest.

*About
the
Author*

BECKY WOODS lives with her husband (Gene) and three children (Heather, Jason & Derrick). They share their house with a Saint Bernard, a Rottweiler, three cats and two chinchillas. She says children might be interested in knowing why she wrote the rabbit story. "My daughter works for a veterinarian who sent two orphaned bunnies home with her for us to care for. At the time we were also bottle feeding a baby raccoon, a baby prairie dog, and frantically digging worms for a baby robin. I researched cottontails to know how to care for them properly and how to prepare them for release once they were old enough to leave our care. The baby rabbits were so enchanting that after watching them, the story of Vila sort of wrote itself. I am very concerned about the future of wildlife and hope that stories about animals will help children develop a concern for them also."

SARAH WOODS considers wildlife art the best of both worlds. Her dedication to both fine art and the wildlife she loves is evident in her work.

Growing up in Wyoming, where she received her Fine Arts degree, she learned early her appreciation of wildlife. That appreciation and knowledge, coupled with Sarah's strong yet sensitive style, have helped her gain both national recognition and acclaim.

Most recently she was invited to participate in the Leigh Yawkey Woodson Museum's *Birds in Art* International Exhibition. She has been included in two *Arts for the Parks* national tours, and numerous other national and international shows. Recent honors include being named Colorado Wildlife Federation's *Artist of the Year*, chosen for inclusion in the National Park Art Collection, as a *Pheasants Forever* Sponsor Print, and winning several *Best of Shows*. Her paintings have appeared on the cover of *Whitetales* and *Waterfowl* USA magazines, and she has been featured in *Wildlife Art News* and *Colorado State* magazines.

Sarah paints in watercolor, gouache, acrylic, and combinations of the the three. Using watermedia allows Sarah to combine delicate transparent washes with the more opaque quality found in her detail work. She tries to blend strong composition, color and design while giving the viewer a privileged glimpse of wildlife.

Sarah enjoys doing field research, photography, and sketching while traveling throughout the Rocky Mountains with her husband, Randy. Their home and *Woodswork Wildlife Art Studio* is located in Fort Collins, Colorado.

Sarah Woods is currently showing at the Trailside Galleries in Jackson, Wyoming, Gallery West in Laramie, Wyoming and Blackhawk Galleries in Saratoga, Wyoming and Tucson, Arizona.